BABY-SITTERS
Little Sister

n's Show and
Share

Ann M. Martin

Illustrations by Susan Crocca Tang

A
LITTLE APPLE
PAPERBACK

SCHOLASTIC INC.
New York Toronto London Auckland Sydney
Mexico City New Delhi Hong Kong

ISBN 0-590-50061-9

Copyright © 1999 by Ann M. Martin. Illustrations copyright © 1999 by Scholastic Inc. All rights reserved. Published by Scholastic Inc. THE BABY-SITTERS LITTLE SISTER, LITTLE APPLE PAPERBACKS, and associated logos are trademarks and/or registered trademarks of Scholastic Inc.

12 11 10 9 8 7 6 5 4 3 2 1   9/9 0 1 2 3 4/0

Printed in the U.S.A.   40
First Scholastic printing, May 1999

*The author gratefully acknowledges
Gabrielle Charbonnet
for her help
with this book.*

Karen's Show and Share

Ms. Colman's Announcement

"Settle down, class," Ms. Colman said. "I would like to make an announcement." Ms. Colman is my teacher. She is the best teacher in the world.

"Oh, goody," I said. I sat up straight in my seat. I love Surprising Announcements.

"As you know, we have been growing flowers in pots for the last couple of months," said Ms. Colman.

I nodded and looked over at the class windowsill. A long row of plastic flowerpots stood there. A beautiful bunch of bright yellow marigolds was in each pot. I could see my pot from where I sat. I thought my flowers seemed especially bright that day.

"Soon we will decorate larger clay pots. Then we will transfer our flowers into the new pots," said Ms. Colman.

"Double goody," I said. I love decorating things. I am very good at it.

"But that is not all. After we are done, we will go to Stoneybrook Manor and give them to the residents," Ms. Colman said.

"Triple goody!" I love visiting Stoney-brook Manor.

Oh, but wait. I have not told you what Stoneybrook Manor is. I have not even told you who I am.

My name is Karen Brewer. I am seven years old and in second grade. I have blonde hair, blue eyes, and freckles. I wear glasses — blue ones for reading and pink ones for the rest of the time.

There is much, much more to know about me. And I will tell all of it to you later. Right now I have to explain about Stoneybrook Manor.

Stoneybrook Manor is a senior citizens' residence. That means it is a home for older people. They go there to live when they cannot take good care of themselves at home.

I like meeting old people. And old people like meeting me. Maybe that is because I am usually cheerful and friendly.

Ms. Colman continued talking. "But there is still more," she said. "The residents of Stoneybrook Manor are interested in what we have been doing since the last time we saw them. So each of you will present a short Show and Share.

"To get ready for our presentations at Stoneybrook Manor, we will practice our Show and Share skills here at school. Tomorrow I would like three students to present Show and Shares. We will work on speaking clearly, smiling, and sharing things that will be interesting to our friends at Stoneybrook Manor."

I love showing and sharing more than practically anything else in the whole world. During Show and Share I get to stand in front of an audience (my class). Everyone has to pay attention to me. It is my chance to shine.

My arm shot up. I looked around. Some other kids had put their hands in the air. I waved my hand around. Since I sit in the front row with the other glasses-wearers, Ms. Colman could not miss me.

"Okay," said Ms. Colman. "I would like Ian Johnson, Addie Sidney, and Karen Brewer to show and share with us tomorrow." She wrote our names in a little book.

I was not sure what comes after "triple goody." So instead, I said "goody" four times: "Goody, goody, goody, goody!"

(Ms. Colman gave me a Look, but she did not remind me to use my indoor voice.)

I was gigundoly excited about visiting Stoneybrook Manor. Already I was planning to come up with a superspecial Show and

Share for our visit — something that would really knock the socks off the residents of Stoneybrook Manor.

But first, I had to practice a little on my classmates. This was going to be fun.

2

The Little House

"I'm home!" I called out when I arrived home at the little house that afternoon. (I will tell you about the little house and the big house in a minute.)

I was expecting someone to call, "Hi, Karen!" That is always nice to hear when I arrive home.

I stood at the front door. No one welcomed me.

Then I listened closely for a second. I heard singing, coming from the kitchen:

"This old man, he played four.
He played knick-knack on my door
With a knick-knack, paddywhack . . ."

It was Merry, my nanny, and Andrew, my little brother. (Andrew is four, going on five.)

I ran into the kitchen. "I'm hoooome!" I called out, extra loudly.

"Oh, Karen, my goodness!" Merry exclaimed. "I did not hear you come in."

"Hi, Karen!" Andrew said. He waved a pretzel stick at me. "Merry and I were singing."

"I know," I said. "I heard."

"Karen, why don't you sit down and have a snack," said Merry. She put a plate of pretzel sticks and apple slices at my place at the table. "You could join us in another round of 'This Old Man.'"

"Okay," I said. I sat down, ate an apple slice, and started singing.

"This old man, he played one.
He played knick-knack on my thumb . . ."

"This Old Man" is not my favorite song of all time. But Andrew likes it, and I had fun singing along with Merry and him.

We knick-knacked all the way up to twelve. Then Andrew wanted to start over at one again. I had had enough knick-knacking, so I did not start over with him. I concentrated on my pretzels instead.

Merry laughed. "Why, Andrew, you certainly love singing. Perhaps I could play the piano for you someday, while you sing."

Andrew stopped singing. "You play the piano, Merry?"

Merry nodded. "Yes, I do play, a little. I enjoy it."

"I wish we had a piano here for you to play," said Andrew.

"There is not enough room in the little house," I pointed out. "The big house would be better."

Okay. I said I would tell you about my big house and my little house. Here is what you need to know.

A long, long time ago, I lived in the big

house all the time. I lived with my mommy, my daddy, and Andrew. Then Mommy and Daddy got divorced. So Andrew and I went to live with Mommy in the little house. (Daddy stayed at the big house. It is the house he grew up in.)

After awhile, Mommy got married again, to a very nice man named Seth Engle. He is my stepfather. So now my little-house family is Mommy, Seth, Andrew, Rocky (Seth's cat), Midgie (Seth's dog), Emily Junior (my pet rat), and Bob (Andrew's hermit crab).

Back at the big house, Daddy got married again too, to Elizabeth Thomas. She already had four children. Sam and Charlie are really old. They go to Stoneybrook High School. Kristy is thirteen and the best stepsister ever. David Michael is seven years old, but he does not go to my school. He goes to Stoneybrook Elementary.

Soon Daddy and Elizabeth adopted my little sister, Emily Michelle, from a country called Vietnam. (Emily is two and a half.) And Elizabeth's mother, Nannie, came to live at the big house to help take care of all the people and pets.

There are many pets at the big house. Shannon is David Michael's Bernese mountain dog puppy. Pumpkin is a little black kitten. Andrew and I have two goldfish, Goldfishie and Crystal Light the Second. And Emily Junior and Bob live at the big house whenever Andrew and I do. So you can see that the big house is pretty full, even though it *is* a big house.

Andrew and I live at the little house every other month, and at the big house in between. This is one of the reasons I call us Andrew Two-Two and Karen Two-Two. I have two of lots of things: houses, families, stuffed cats, bicycles, beds. I even have a nanny (Merry) and a Nannie!

I also have two best friends, Hannie Papadakis and Nancy Dawes. Hannie lives across the street and one house down from the big house. Nancy lives next door to the little house. We are all in Ms. Colman's class. We call ourselves the Three Musketeers. Our motto is "All for one, and one for all!"

Andrew was just finishing up the last verse of "This Old Man":

"... *With a knick-knack, paddywhack,*
    Give a dog a bone.
This old man came rolling ho-o-ome!"

"One more time!" shouted Andrew, waving his spoon.

Merry laughed. "Andrew, if you love music so much, maybe you should learn to play an instrument."

Andrew's eyes grew wide. "Play an instrument? Like the piano? Wow? What a great idea! I would love to know how to play an instrument."

"Well, since you do not have a piano in the house, it would be a little hard to learn how to play one," said Merry. "But I am sure we can find some other instrument for you."

"Oh, boy! That would be great, Merry!" said Andrew.

For some reason, I was not excited about Andrew learning to play an instrument. I had a feeling it was going to be more fun for him than it would be for anyone else.

3

Show and Share

The next morning at breakfast I remembered that I had to present a Show and Share to my class that day.

I was worried. I would not need to practice my Show and Share ahead of time. It is easy for me to talk in front of the class. I do not get nervous. I could make it up as I went along. Still, I had to bring in something to talk about. Something interesting, but not the superinteresting thing I would save for Stoneybrook Manor. (I did not know what that was yet. But I knew I could come up

14

with something.) Today I thought about bring-ing in Tickly, my special blanket. Or Goosie, my stuffed cat.

As I thought, I poured myself another bowl of Krispy Krunchie cereal. A piece of cardboard inside a clear plastic wrapper fell into my bowl. A Krispy Krunchie surprise!

I fished out the surprise. I wiped milk and Krispy Krunchie dust off of it with my nap-kin. Then I ripped open the plastic. Inside was a baseball card!

I looked at the picture of the player. He was holding a baseball bat and smiling. He looked friendly. The card said his name was Bobby Martinez.

I like surprises. I liked my new baseball card. And I knew what I was going to show and share with my class that day.

"Last year my mommy went on a busi-ness trip to Washington State," said Ian Johnson during Show and Share that day. "She visited Mount St. Helens, the volcano that blew up years ago."

Ian held up a black rock about the size of a baked potato.

"Mommy picked up this rock from the slope of Mount St. Helens," he said. "It is a chunk of cooled lava, straight from the volcano."

I oohed and ahhed. So did all the other kids in the class. A real volcano rock! That is a pretty good Show and Share.

Ian handed the rock to Ricky Torres, my pretend husband, to look at. (Ricky and I got married on the playground one day.) Ricky held the rock carefully and looked at it. I heard Ricky whisper, "Wow! Real lava!" Then he passed it to the kid in back of him.

Ian talked some more about Mount St. Helens. When he was finished, everyone clapped.

Addie was next. She rolled to the front of the class in her wheelchair.

"Today I would like to show you some artwork I made on my computer at home," began Addie. She explained how she had a new program that let her draw pictures with a mouse right on the screen. She could color the pictures, as if she were using markers on paper. Plus, once the drawing was made, she could ask the program to change the drawing in lots of different ways. She held up some pieces of paper to show us what she meant.

"This is a printout of my first drawing," said Addie. It was a picture of a cat lying on a windowsill. Through the window you could see a tree and the sun. (It was very nice. Addie is an excellent artist.) The drawing looked as if it had been done in crayon.

"This is a printout of the same picture," said Addie. "Only this time, I asked the computer to make it look like a watercolor painting."

She held up another piece of paper. It was the same drawing of a cat in a window. But this one looked as if it had been done in watercolors.

All the kids oohed and ahhed. So did I. It was pretty cool. I wondered if Daddy would get me that art program for the computer at the big house.

Then Addie showed us the same picture printed out in several more ways — as a chalk drawing, a black-and-white drawing, and even as a stained-glass window!

Addie handed all the pictures to Ricky. (Like me, Ricky sits in the front row because he wears glasses. That is why he was handed things first.) He looked carefully at each piece of paper. I heard him whisper, "Wow! This is really neat!"

Addie finished up her Show and Share. Everyone clapped.

"Karen, are you ready for Show and Share?" asked Ms. Colman.

"Yes," I said. I walked to the front of the classroom. I held up my baseball card.

"This is a baseball card," I said. "The player is Bobby Martinez. He plays for . . ." I glanced at the card. "He plays for the San Diego Padres." I waved the card so everyone could see it. A baseball card, especially a brand-new one, is pretty neat, I thought.

The class looked interested. But they did not look *very* interested.

I did not have any more to say. I had shown the card. I had shared just about all I knew about it. No one was oohing and ahhing, though. Hmm, I thought. Maybe my class wanted something more.

I glanced at the card again. On the back were some facts about the player. Very convenient, I thought. "Bobby Martinez is an outfielder," I said. "He is a really good player." (I did not know if that was true. I figured it must be, if he was on a card.)

Still no oohing or ahhing.

My classmates looked less interested than they had before. Terri Barkan was fidgeting. Jannie Gilbert was doodling on a piece of scrap paper. Ricky, my pretend husband, had his mouth wide open in a yawn.

My Show and Share was flopping! I had to do something, and fast. But what?

"I found this card in a box of Krispy Krunchies," I said.

No one seemed impressed. I was still flopping.

What else could I say about it? What would make it a better Show and Share? My classmates were a tough audience. I could not stand it. I wanted them to ooh and ahh, the way I had done for them.

Suddenly I blurted out, "I have met Bobby Martinez." I do not know where that came from. It just popped out of my mouth.

Terri stopped fidgeting.

"I have met him more than once," I said, listening to myself in amazement.

Jannie looked up from her doodle.

"He is a friend of mine," I went on. My eyes were wide. My heart was pounding. What was I doing?

Ricky's mouth was still open. But he was not yawning anymore. His mouth was open in wonder.

"Bobby Martinez has been to my house,"

I said. It was like watching a horrible accident happen before your eyes. I could not stop myself. When I looked into the amazed and impressed faces of my classmates, I was happy. Now everyone was paying attention. My Show and Share was no longer a flop. I was a gigundo success!

4

Lies

"Here," I said. I handed Ricky my baseball card, so he could pass it around.

I waited for everyone to applaud my Show and Share. Then I would just sit down and it would be over.

Instead, hands shot up all over the room, and kids started shouting questions at me.

"How do you know Bobby Martinez?" "When did he come to your house?" "What did you have for dinner?" "Did Bobby have seconds?"

There were too many questions at once. I

could not answer them all. (Actually, I could not answer any of them.)

I held up my hands. "Settle down, class, please," I said. "Indoor voices, people!" I have always wanted to say that. (I bet Ms. Colman thinks it's fun too.)

When everyone had stopped yelling, I said, "My Show and Share is over. You may ask me about Bobby Martinez during recess."

By recess, I figured, they would have forgotten about my baseball card. Or I would have thought of a story to explain how I knew Bobby Martinez.

"Bobby Martinez is my favorite player of all time," said Ricky. "How long have you known him?"

"What is he like?" asked Omar Harris.

"Is he nice?" asked Jannie.

Guess what. They had not forgotten. During the last hour I had thought about telling my friends the truth at recess. But I did not want them to know I had lied. So now I found myself answering questions about someone I had never met!

"Bobby is very nice," I said. I tried to sound as if I knew what I was talking about.

"Wow," said Ricky. "Cool."

"How do you know him?" asked Jannie.

"Um, Bobby Martinez is an old friend of my stepfather, Seth," I said. "They knew each other in high school, before Bobby was a big star. They were on the baseball team together. They were practically best friends."

(I know high schools have baseball teams because my stepbrother Charlie is on one.)

"Wow," said Ricky. "Teammates. Way cool."

"Yes, it is way cool," I said.

"So, he has been to your house?" asked Omar.

I nodded helplessly.

"You ate dinner with him?" he asked.

I nodded again.

"What did he eat?" asked Jannie.

What had I had for dinner the night before?

"Pizza," I said. "Bobby loves pizza. He had four large slices."

"Four? Gosh," said Omar.

"With extra cheese," I said.

"Well, Bobby is a big guy," said Ricky. "He would have a big appetite."

I nodded. "That is right."

"So, Karen, have you ever been to Bobby's house?" asked Jannie.

Uh-oh. I did not even know where Bobby Martinez lived. Would it be San Diego, where his team played? I had no idea.

I decided it would be safer to say I had not been to his house. Then I would not have to describe it.

"No, I have never been to his house," I said. By the looks on their faces, I could tell they were disappointed. "But Seth has," I added quickly. "They are still really good friends. Seth visits him sometimes. We have pictures of Bobby in our family photo album."

"Oooh," said Ricky.

"But I have not visited Bobby at his house," I added. "After all, he plays for the San Diego Padres, and I have never been to San Diego. It is very far away from Stoneybrook, you know. But I will probably visit him someday."

For two seconds, Ricky, Omar, and Jannie said nothing. It was my chance to get away.

"Hi!" I shouted over to Hannie and Nancy. They were getting ready to climb the jungle gym. "I will be right there," I called.

"Well," I said to Ricky, Omar, and Jannie, "I have to be going now. It was fun talking about Bobby Martinez with you guys. See you later."

I ran off toward the jungle gym as quickly as my legs would take me.

5

Bugle Boy

When I got home that afternoon, I was exhausted. (Making up lies is hard work.)

All I wanted to do was lie down on the couch, close my eyes, and rest. Maybe while I was resting I could think up a way to make Bobby Martinez disappear from my life.

Blaaaat!

My eyes flew open.

Blaaaat!

Andrew was standing next to me. He was blowing into some sort of horn.

Blaaaat!

28

"This is a bugle," said Andrew. "Isn't it great?" He took a deep breath. *Blaaaat!*

"It is not great," I said. "It is horrible. Why do you keep making that horrible noise with that horrible horn?"

"It is not horrible noise," said Andrew. *Blaaaat!* "It is pretty music." *Blaaaat!*

I was about to tell Andrew to go make pretty music someplace else. Of all days, I was definitely not in the mood for Andrew's "music." But Merry came into the room before I had a chance.

"Karen, come have a snack," she said firmly. She crooked her finger at me.

"Sure," I muttered. "Anything to get away from this — "

Blaaaat!

I followed Merry to the kitchen.

"Now Karen, I want you to be nice to Andrew about his bugle playing," said Merry. "He is showing an interest in music. We should encourage him."

"But it is so loud," I said.

Merry gave me a Look.

"Why the bugle?" I asked. "Why can't Andrew play a quieter instrument? Like — a triangle?"

"After Andrew said he wanted to learn about music, I asked your mother and Seth if they had any musical instruments," Merry explained. "The only one they had was Seth's old bugle. When he was a camp counselor years ago, he used to play it at sunup and sundown."

"I wish Seth had played the flute," I said.

"Be nice," Merry told me. "Andrew has been having fun with his bugle. Let's not spoil it for him."

"Okay," I said. "I will be nice."

"Promise?"

"I promise."

Just then Andrew came running into the kitchen.

Blaaaaaat!

"Wow, did you hear that?" he said.

Merry and I nodded. How could we not have heard it? Daddy and Nannie, in the big house across town, probably heard it.

"Very nice," I said miserably.

I looked at Merry. She smiled at me.

"Thank you," said Andrew.

Blaaaat!

I decided to lie down in my room. My head was starting to hurt.

6

To Tell the Truth

By the next morning, I hoped that my classmates would be thinking about something other than Bobby Martinez. No such luck. Bobby Martinez was all anyone wanted to talk about.

Bobby Martinez this, Bobby Martinez that.

If only I had not gotten that baseball card out of the box of Krispy Krunchies! I had been hoping for some cool butterfly tattoos. They would not have caused me nearly as much trouble.

For the rest of the week I tried not to answer any more questions about Bobby Martinez. I kept ducking and dodging and making myself look busy. Luckily, my two best friends were not pestering me about Bobby Martinez. In fact, Hannie and Nancy had not mentioned him at all. They do not care very much about baseball.

But on Friday things got worse.

I was hanging upside down on the jungle gym during recess. Ricky appeared and stood next to me.

"Hi, Karen," he said.

I swung through my arms and landed on my feet. (This is a fancy move that I have practiced a lot. It looks harder than it is.)

"Hi, Ricky," I replied. I wanted to distract him before he could ask me about you-know-who. "Have you heard the latest song by the Lemon Drops? I am going to buy their new — "

"Karen, do you think you could please do me a really big, really special favor?" Ricky asked.

34

Now, when a person asks politely for a favor, it is hard to say no. When that person is your pretend husband, it is almost impossible. Still, I wanted to know what the favor was before I agreed to it.

"What kind of favor?" I asked.

"Well, you are good friends with Bobby Martinez," said Ricky.

Uh-oh.

"And I am good friends with you," said Ricky. "In fact, I am your pretend husband. Right?"

I nodded slowly. "Right."

"Well, do you think Bobby Martinez could visit our class someday?" he asked.

"Oh, I do not think so," I said confidently. "He is a very busy man. Baseball season has started already. And it does not end until . . . " I did not know when it ended exactly. "Well, until a very long time from now."

"Oh," said Ricky. He looked disappointed.

I felt bad letting my pretend husband down. I wanted to make him feel better.

36

"Sorry," I said. "But you know how it is. He is playing baseball almost every day. Even Seth hardly hears from him during baseball season."

"Oh," said Ricky, looking very sad. "It is just that Bobby Martinez is my favorite player in the whole world. I liked him even when he was a rookie. I think he is terrific. If I met him, it would be the best thing that could ever happen to me."

"Is there something else I could do?" I asked.

"Well," said Ricky, scuffling his sneaker in the dirt. Suddenly his face brightened. My stomach knotted up. "Hey! I know!" said Ricky. "Maybe you could get an autographed picture of Bobby Martinez for me. You probably have a stack of them at home, since he is such good friends with Seth. Could I have one, please?"

"Uh . . ." I said. I had no idea how to get an autographed picture of a baseball star. Could I buy one at a store?

"It would mean a lot to me, Karen," said

Ricky. "It would be just about the best thing anyone ever did for me."

Ricky gave me a big, sweet smile.

How could I say no?

"I will see," I said. "I will ask Seth about it. I know we do not have any at home right now, but maybe Seth could give Bobby a call." I wanted to melt into the ground as I said that.

"Thanks, Karen!" said Ricky happily. "You are the best pretend wife ever."

I smiled weakly. "No problem," I said.

I was trapped.

7

Letter to Bobby

The next week was one long nightmare. I spent every day dodging Ricky and the other kids at school. They still had questions about Bobby Martinez. It was all I could do to keep one step ahead of them.

At home, Andrew had, thank goodness, given up on the bugle. (I guess he finally realized that *blaaaat*s are not the same thing as music.) But he had taken up a new instrument. And you will find this hard to believe, but it was even worse than the bugle.

Andrew had discovered the tom-tom drum.

Thugga-thugga-thugga-thugga, went Andrew on the drum. Over and over. For hours at a time.

Thugga-thugga-thugga-thugga, *thugga-thugga-thugga-thugga.* I heard it first thing in the morning. *Thugga-thugga-thugga-thugga.* I heard it at breakfast. *Thugga-thugga-thugga-thugga.* I heard it when I got home from school. *Thugga-thugga-thugga-thugga.* I heard it after dinner. *Thugga-thugga-thugga-thugga.* I heard it in my dreams.

It was enough to make me wish for the good old days of *blaaaat.*

I tried to complain to Merry. "Andrew is driving me bananas with that thugga-thugga-thugging."

"I know," said Merry. "But it is wonderful that Andrew is interested in music. We should all try to be supportive of him."

"I like music," I said. "But banging on a tom-tom does not count as music. It counts as noise."

Merry gave me a Look.

I sighed. "I know," I said. "I will be nice."

"Thank you," said Merry.

I did not like lying to my friends at school. I did not like having to change the subject whenever the name Bobby Martinez came up. I wished I had not lied in the first place. But now that I had, I had to stick with my story.

When I first dumped the Bobby Martinez card out of the box of Krispy Krunchies, I did not really know who he was. But ever since I had claimed I knew him, I had noticed his name everywhere — on TV, on the covers of magazines, in the newspaper.

I had learned a lot about him. For instance, I knew he played right field. I knew he hit a lot of home runs. I knew his favorite cereal was Krispy Krunchies.

And he seemed like a very nice guy. I began to think that if I wrote him a letter and explained what I had done, maybe — just maybe — he would come to my school and pretend to be my friend.

I took out a sheet of paper and sat down to write him the letter.

DEAR BOBBY MARTINEZ,
YOU WILL NEVER GUESS THE DUMB THING I DID THE OTHER DAY.

Hmmm. That was not a good beginning. Bobby Martinez was probably too busy to play guessing games. I crumpled up the paper, took out a new sheet, and started over.

DEAR BOBBY MARTINEZ,
YOU ARE SUPPOSED TO BE MY FRIEND, BUT YOU DO NOT EVEN KNOW WHO I AM.

No, that was not good. It sounded like I was blaming him. I crumpled the paper and started over again.

DEAR BOBBY MARTINEZ,

LET ME START AT THE BEGINNING. ONE MORNING I OPENED A BOX OF KRISPIE KRUNCHIES (THEY ARE MY FAVORITE TOO) AND YOUR CARD FELL OUT. WELL, TO MAKE A LONG STORY SHORT, I NEED YOU TO COME TO MY SCHOOL AND PRETEND WE ARE OLD FRIENDS, SO THAT ALL MY FRIENDS WILL STILL LIKE ME.

YOUR FUTURE OLD FRIEND,
KAREN BREWER

I reread the letter. It sounded terrible. It sounded like I wanted him to be my friend only to help me out. I would hate to get a letter like that.

I thought about the kind of letter I would like to get if I were a big baseball star. Then I took out a clean sheet of paper and wrote:

DEAR BOBBY MARTINEZ,

MY NAME IS KAREN BREWER. I AM SEVEN YEARS OLD. YOU ARE MY FAVORITE BASEBALL PLAYER OF ALL TIME. I LIKE IT WHEN YOU HIT HOME RUNS. BUT YOU WOULD BE MY FAVORITE PLAYER EVEN IF YOU STRUCK

OUT EVERY TIME. THAT IS HOW MUCH I LIKE YOU. I
HOPE YOU HAVE A GOOD SEASON.
   YOUR NUMBER-ONE FAN,
    KAREN BREWER

I reread the letter. I liked it. I had not
asked Bobby to come to my school and pretend to know me. I had only told the truth.
And telling the truth felt good.

I folded up the letter and stuck it in an envelope. I would put it in the mailbox in the
morning.

8

Paints and Pots

"Here is a picture of me during my family's trip to New York," said Omar. He held up a photograph. It showed him standing with one arm raised, like the Statue of Liberty. In the background was the real Statue of Liberty.

It had been two weeks since my Show and Share about Bobby Martinez. We were still practicing our Show and Shares. (Ms. Colman wanted us to be really ready when we went to Stoneybrook Manor.)

"We went to a baseball game when we

were in New York," said Omar. "We saw the Mets play the San Diego Padres. Karen's Bobby Martinez hit the game-winning home run for the Padres."

I cringed. Just when the kids were beginning to forget about Bobby Martinez, Omar had to go and bring him up again.

Omar passed around the photo of him and the Statue of Liberty, then sat down. Everyone clapped.

Ricky was next. He walked to the front of class and held up a book. I could read the title. It was called *Superduperstar: The Bobby Martinez Story*.

"I have been reading a very interesting book," said Ricky. "It is about Karen's friend Bobby Martinez. I can hardly put it down. I am already halfway through chapter three. I cannot wait to see if the book mentions Seth Engle."

Ricky looked at me and smiled.

I tried to smile back. But I could not. I wanted to disappear.

Natalie Springer gave her Show and

Share next, and she did not mention Bobby Martinez, thank goodness. (She showed her penny collection. She has a penny from 1971. That is practically ancient.)

After Show and Share, we worked on decorating our flowerpots. I sat at a table with Hannie and Nancy.

"Too bad Omar did not tell you he was going to see a Padres game," said Nancy. "You could have helped him meet Bobby Martinez."

"Yeah," I said. "That is too bad."

I hated lying to one of my best friends. But I was too ashamed to tell her the truth.

"Funny that you never mentioned Bobby Martinez to us, Karen," said Hannie. She looked at me knowingly.

"Um, yeah, funny," I said.

Luckily, Hannie did not say anything more about Bobby Martinez. I had a feeling she did not really want to catch me in a lie.

I concentrated on decorating my flowerpot. I cut some pink and purple flowers out of construction paper and glued them to the

pot. I added some green construction paper stems and leaves. Then, as an extra touch, I glued on some yellow squiggles that looked like the sun's rays.

I held up my pot. It was very pretty. I could not wait to transplant my flower into it. Then it would be perfect.

In fact, everything about school would be perfect, if it weren't for Bobby Martinez.

9

Karen's Promises

On the way to the bus after school, Ricky caught up to me.

"Karen, wait," he said. "Have you asked Bobby Martinez for his autograph yet?"

"Well, not exactly," I said. "I have not seen him lately."

"How often does he come to your house?" Ricky asked.

"Oh, all the time," I said. "He sometimes comes at holidays."

"That is probably when your family takes the pictures of him, right?" said Ricky.

"Right." Family pictures? Had I said something about family pictures? I kind of remembered saying something about that.

"Do you think you could bring in your photo album, so I could see your pictures of Bobby?" Ricky asked.

"Well, I do not think I would be allowed to bring in our photo album," I said. "My mother would not want me to lose it."

"Oh," said Ricky. "Then I could come over to your house sometime and take a look at it there."

"No!" I said. I thought fast. "You don't have to do that. I think I can bring in a picture of Bobby. Just not the whole family album."

Oh for goodness sake! I was digging myself into a deeper and deeper hole. Where was I going to get a picture of Bobby Martinez with my family?

"That would be great, Karen," said Ricky. He gave me a big smile. "I am really looking forward to seeing it."

*   *   *

51

That evening I looked through all our photo albums, plus a box full of extra pictures. (It was fun. I love looking at pictures of myself when I was small.) I was not looking for a picture of Bobby Martinez, of course. I knew we did not have any of those.

Finally I found what I was looking for. It was a picture taken last Christmas. It showed Andrew, Mommy, Seth, and me. Standing next to Seth was another man. Maybe it was Uncle James. Uncle James is not really an uncle, but just an old friend of Seth's. I could not tell for sure whether it was him because his head was cut off by the edge of the photo. I could not tell who it was.

And if I could not tell whether it was Uncle James, then Ricky would not be able to tell whether it was Bobby Martinez. Which was who I was planning on telling him it was. He would just have to take my word for it.

"This is Bobby Martinez?" asked Ricky.

It was the next day, during recess. Ricky

was holding the photo of my family and Uncle James. He turned the picture this way and that.

"It does not really look like him," Ricky said.

"How can you tell?" I asked. "His head is cut off."

"Bobby Martinez has great big muscles," said Ricky. "From hitting all those home runs. The man in this picture is skinny."

"Well, I do not know about that," I said. "This was at Christmas, you know. Baseball players do not play during the winter. Maybe Bobby lost some weight during the off-season."

"Hmm," said Ricky. "Maybe." He handed me back the picture. "Anyway, Karen, I was wondering if you could please, please, please do me one more huge, gigantic, enormous favor."

I had a bad feeling about this. I had already found him a picture. What now?

Ricky reached into the pocket of his

windbreaker. He pulled out a brand-new, shiny white baseball.

"I took all the money out of my bank and bought this baseball," Ricky explained. "It is an official Major League ball, just like the ones Bobby Martinez knocks out of the park."

Ricky handed the ball to me.

"What do you want me to do with it?" I asked him. I was afraid of the answer.

"It would be the best thing anyone ever did for me ever," said Ricky, "if you could have Bobby Martinez sign it for me."

I nodded. Then I sighed long and hard.

"I will see what I can do," I said glumly.

10

Easy as Pie

That afternoon I went home in a bad mood. How was I going to get Ricky's baseball autographed by Bobby Martinez? I could not even come up with an auto-graphed picture.

Note to myself, I thought: Do not ever make anything up ever again for the rest of your life. You will regret it.

When I came in the front door to the little house, I heard a weird sort of humming-warbling sound. At first I thought Andrew had taken up the bugle again. Then I realized that whatever was making the noise was not a bugle.

"I am home! What is that racket?" I shouted as I hung up my jacket in the hall closet.

Merry came into the living room from the kitchen. "Now Karen, be — "

Waaa-waaa-waaa, waaa-waaa-waaa!

Andrew came charging down the stairs, holding something up to his mouth. It was making the humming-warbling sound. I recognized the tune — it was "This Old Man" again.

And I recognized what he was playing it on.

It was a kazoo.

"Look, Karen!" Andrew shouted. He stuck the kazoo back in his mouth and blew.

Waaa-waaa-waaa, waaa-waaa-waaa!

"All you have to do is hum into it, and it makes real music," Andrew said. "See? Easy as pie."

He gave me another demonstration.

I was about to say something when Merry gave me a Look.

"That is great, Andrew," I muttered.

"It is much easier than the bugle," Andrew said. "I could not really play the bugle very well."

"Oh really?" I asked, as if I had not noticed.

"And the tom-tom was a little boring," he added. "It was just the same thing over and over."

I nodded but did not say anything. (Mommy says that if you cannot say anything nice, do not say anything at all.)

"But the kazoo is perfect," Andrew went on. "It is not hard to play. Any tune I can hum, I can play on the kazoo."

"Gosh," I said. "Any tune at all?" This was not good news.

"Yes," said Andrew. "From now on, I am going to practice the kazoo twenty-four hours a day!"

I smiled weakly. I took a deep breath.

"Wonderful," I said.

Andrew turned and marched away, kazooing "This Old Man."

I said to Merry, "The kazoo? Whose idea was that?"

"Your mother, Seth, and I thought that the kazoo would be an improvement over the bugle and the tom-tom," Merry explained. "I took him to the toy store this morning to pick one up. He loves his new kazoo. And it is better than the tom-tom, don't you think?"

I did not answer right away. I had to think about it.

Finally I said, "I am not sure. I have to think about it."

And I left it at that.

11

Lying to Charlie

I went up to my room and closed the door. Through the wall I could hear the sound of "This Old Man" on the kazoo. I knew I would start to hate that song soon. I played a CD to drown out the noise.

Then I lay on my bed and took Ricky's baseball out of my backpack. Think, think, think. How could I possibly get it autographed by Bobby Martinez? Mail it to him and ask him to sign it and send it back? I doubted that would work, and besides, it would take too long. Bobby was supposed to be a friend of mine.

An idea popped into my mind. Maybe I could just sign the ball myself with Bobby's name. Ricky might never know the difference. It was an awful thing to do, but I had done some other awful things already. How much worse could this be?

I took out a sheet of paper and a pen and practiced signing Bobby's name:

I looked at the signature and frowned. It did not look like the signature of a big, tough professional ballplayer. It looked like the signature of a seven-year-old.

I wrote his name again, this time trying to make my writing look older:

Bobby Martinez

I looked at what I had written and frowned again. It looked like the signature of a seven-year-old who was pretending to be a big, tough professional ballplayer. There was no way that Ricky would be fooled by it.

I did not want Ricky (and everyone else) to find out that I had lied about knowing Bobby Martinez. But I also did not want to let him down. Ricky would be thrilled to have Bobby Martinez's autograph. I did not want him to be disappointed.

Just then the phone rang. I dashed out of my room and answered it.

"Hello," I said.

"Hi, Karen," said the voice at the other end. "This is Elizabeth. Your father and I are going to have a backyard cookout on Saturday afternoon. We were wondering if you and Andrew would like to join us."

"A barbecue party?" I said. "That sounds great! I would love to come."

"Good," said Elizabeth. "We will see you then."

"Okay," I said. "I will be looking forward to it."

I hung up the phone.

I love cookouts at the big house. The food is always delicious, and we always play Frisbee and tag and catch. Even Sam and Charlie play, and they are usually too old to play with me. They are practically grown up. . . .

I tossed Ricky's ball in the air and caught it. Then I froze like a statue. I had just thought of something. Charlie was almost a grown-up. He was big and tough. (Not as big and tough as Bobby Martinez, but still, he was *fairly* big and tough.) He played baseball.

Charlie's signature would look as if it could be Bobby Martinez's.

The only question was, how could I get Charlie to sign Bobby's name on Ricky's ball?

As soon as the last chicken leg was picked clean on Saturday afternoon, I called to Sam and Charlie for a game of catch.

"I have an idea," I said. "Let's pretend to be our favorite players." I slapped Ricky's baseball into my glove. "I will be Tom Triplett Jr." (Tom Triplett Jr. was a player I had heard of.)

"I will be Gary Westover," said Sam. "He is a great pitcher."

Charlie said, "I will be — "

"Bobby Martinez!" I shouted. "Charlie will be Bobby Martinez! You are probably just as good a player as he is."

Charlie laughed. "Well, okay, Karen, if you say so. I will be Bobby Martinez."

We tossed the ball around for a few minutes. Then I threw to Charlie high up in the air. He leaped up and snagged it.

"Wow!" I cried. "Great catch, Char — I mean, Bobby." I ran to Charlie. "Oh, Bobby, Bobby! I am your biggest fan!" I pulled a felt-tip pen out of my pocket. "Could you please, please sign the baseball?" I shoved the pen into his hand. "Pretty please?"

Charlie was laughing. "You want my au-

tograph? Okay, sure. Should I sign it, 'To Karen, from Charlie'?"

"No!" I shouted. "You are Bobby Martinez, remember? Just sign his name — nothing else. Okay?"

Charlie gave me a funny look. Then he shrugged and said, "Okay."

He signed the ball and handed it to me.

It looked great. Ricky would *have* to believe that Bobby Martinez had signed the ball.

"Oh, thank you, thank you, Bobby!" I said, clutching the ball to my chest. "I will keep it forever and ever."

"You are welcome, kid," said Charlie.

I ran off to put the ball away. The game of catch was over. I would give the ball to Ricky on Monday. Then he would stop bugging me.

I felt a little bad about tricking Charlie. But he would never know what I had done. And I had done it for a good cause.

Sort of. It was getting hard for me to tell.

Ricky's Baseball

"Ri-i-i-icky," I called. "Come he-e-e-ere."

It was Monday morning, before school had started. We were on the playground. For the first time in awhile, I was actually happy to go to school.

Ricky ran to me. "What is it, Karen?" he asked.

"Guess what I have behind my back," I said.

"Umm," said Ricky thoughtfully, "a jump rope?"

"Nope."

"A banana?"

"Nope."

"A rock?"

"Nope." I laughed. "Give up?"

"Yup," said Ricky. "Now show me what you have behind your back."

Slowly, very, very slowly, I brought my hand around to my front. I held the ball up.

Ricky's eyes went wide.

"Oh. Man," he said slowly. "Is that what I think it is?"

"Yup," I said. "It is Bobby Martinez's autograph."

"Wow!" said Ricky. "Can I hold it?"

"Sure," I said. I handed him the ball. "You can hold it. It is yours."

I do not think a pretend husband has ever been more grateful to his pretend wife. Ricky must have thanked me about two hundred times.

"It was nothing," I said modestly. "Do not mention it."

And that was the truth. I did not want him to mention it ever again.

Unfortunately, he did mention it. The very next day. And this time, he was not thanking me. He was yelling at me.

"This is not Bobby Martinez's signature!" he said.

I pretended I did not know what he was talking about.

"Not Bobby Martinez's signature?" I asked. "Why, what do you mean?"

"Yesterday after school I took the ball you gave me to the baseball card shop at the mall," Ricky said. "They sell autographed stuff down there, and they know how to spot a fake. They said that this is definitely not Bobby Martinez's autograph. What do you have to say to that, Karen?"

I did not know what to say.

"Um, uh," I sputtered.

"Well?" Ricky crossed his arms over his chest.

"I guess Bobby asked his secretary to sign the ball," I said. "Bobby is a very busy man, you know. He probably has a secretary who does a lot of things for him, like sign baseballs. Yes, now it is coming back to me. Seth, who is practically Bobby's best friend, once mentioned to me that Bobby has a secretary who does that kind of thing for him."

I waited for Ricky to say something. But he did not. He just pushed the baseball into my hand, turned, and walked away.

13

The Kazoo Kid

On Wednesday afternoon Hannie and Nancy came to the little house. We sat in my room, playing Lovely Ladies. I was happy to be playing a normal game with friends who could not care less about Bobby Martinez.

"Dahling, more tea, please," I said in my best Lovely Lady voice.

Nancy pretended to refill my cup. "Cucumber sandwich, dear?"

"No thank you, dahling. I filled up on the watercress sandwiches."

Suddenly a horrible racket filled the room.

Hannie fluttered her hand against her chest. "What *is* that dreadful noise?" she asked.

Nancy said, "It sounds like an animal howling 'This Old Man.' "

"Close," I muttered. "It is Andrew. On the kazoo. But you were right about 'This Old Man.' "

"Can you tell him to stop?" Hannie asked in her regular, non-Lovely voice. "Or at least go away?"

"No," I said sadly. "He is allowed to practice in his room. In fact, it is the only room where he is allowed to practice."

"I can understand why," said Hannie. "His playing is terrible."

"And he does it *all the time*," I said. "I have tried everything to block out the noise — cotton in my ears, earmuffs, a pillow tied around my head. But that kazoo manages to get through everything. Even in my sleep, I can hear 'This Old Man.' And sometimes

he plays other songs! Songs I used to like. I will never like them again."

My friends gave me a sorry look.

Hannie patted my hand and said in her Lovely Lady voice, "We must be strong, dear."

"Drink some more tea, dahling," said Nancy, pretending to fill up my cup again. "And have a cucumber sandwich. It will do you good."

14

Superduperstar

Friday was a clear, sunny, warm, beautiful spring day. I skipped around the blacktop at school.

"Karen," I heard someone call.

I stopped skipping. Ricky was walking toward me.

Uh-oh. I started skipping again. Ricky picked up his pace, until he was flat-out running. He caught up to me.

"Karen," he said. "Didn't you hear me calling you?"

I stopped skipping. "Oh, hi, Ricky," I said.

"I want to talk to you about something." Ricky pulled a book out of his backpack. It was *Superduperstar: The Bobby Martinez Story*.

"I finished my book on Bobby Martinez," he said. "And I was wondering about some of the things you said about him."

"Oh," I said. I could feel my face turning red. I had a feeling that some of the things I had said about Bobby might not have been quite accurate. "Like what?"

"Well, the book says that Bobby grew up in the Dominican Republic," said Ricky. "I asked my dad where that is, and he said it is on an island in the Caribbean. They speak Spanish there."

"Really?" I said, trying to act cool.

"Yes," said Ricky. "You said your stepfather went to high school with Bobby. I did not know your stepfather was from the Dominican Republic. I thought he was American."

"Oh!" I thought fast. "Well, Seth is American. He was born here. He only lived in the

Dominican Republic for a little while. During high school."

Ricky gave me a funny look.

"It says here" — he pointed at the book — "that Bobby Martinez is twenty-six years old. Isn't your stepfather older than that? How could he have gone to high school with Bobby?"

I flushed. "Oh, uh, did I say they were players on the same team?" I asked. Now I really had to think quickly. "No, I did not. I meant to say that Seth was the *coach* of Bobby's high school baseball team. Um, yes, sure, that is it. Seth lived in the Dominican Republic for awhile, coaching baseball. That is where he met Bobby. They became friends. Right."

"Right," Ricky repeated. He had a look on his face that said one thing: *I know you are lying.*

"I have another question," said Ricky. "You said Bobby ate pizza at your house."

I nodded. "He had four slices."

"According to this book," said Ricky,

"Bobby is allergic to milk. He never eats cheese. It makes him sick. So how could he eat pizza at your house, Karen?"

I gritted my teeth. "We had a special kind of pizza with no cheese on top," I shot back.

"Well, you said before that there was extra cheese. Now you say there was no cheese. Fine. But what about this?" Ricky went on. He was becoming very angry. "You said that you had never been to Bobby's house, because he plays for the San Diego Padres."

"That is correct," I said. The baseball card I got out of Krispie Krunchies showed him in a San Diego uniform.

"But this is his very first season as a Padre," Ricky said. "He was traded at the end of last year from the Chicago Cubs. He still has a house in Chicago. You were in Chicago last fall. Why didn't you visit him then? Huh, Karen? Why didn't you? Was it because your stepfather is not best friends with him? Was it because you have not, in fact, even *met* Bobby Martinez?"

I did not like the way my pretend hus-

band was treating me. I was becoming very upset. The beautiful spring morning was ruined.

"I — I — " I started to say. But I could not think of anything. Ricky had found me out. He knew I was lying.

"I think you are being very mean, Ricky Torres!" I shouted. Then I burst into tears and ran away.

15

Two Families

I avoided Ricky for the rest of that day. He avoided me too.

Over the weekend, I thought and thought about what I should do about Ricky. He was sure to tell the other kids that I had lied. There was nothing I could do to stop him. I would just have to face the music. I groaned to myself. At school I had to face the music of everyone knowing I had lied. At home I had to face Andrew's music. Things were horrible everywhere I went.

On Monday after school Hannie and

Nancy came over for another Lovely Ladies party. After tea and crumpets, we decided to rehearse our upcoming Show and Share presentations. I was definitely going to rehearse a good Show and Share, a real one, and be totally ready.

This was the week my class was going to Stoneybrook Manor. Ms. Colman had divided the class into three groups. The first would visit on Tuesday, the second on Wednesday, and the third on Thursday. (I was in the second group. Hannie and Nancy were in the third group.)

Since I would be the first of the Three Musketeers to go to Stoneybrook Manor, I rehearsed my Show and Share first.

I stood up and said in a loud, clear voice, "My name is Karen Brewer. The title of my Show and Share is 'My Two Families.' " I smiled.

I held up two photographs — one of my little-house family, and one of my big-house family. The pictures were the *show* part of my Show and Share.

I said that I had two families, with two mommies and two daddies. I talked about going back and forth between the big house and the little house with Andrew. I said that sometimes it is a little difficult, but mostly it is a fine way to grow up.

When I was finished, I took a bow.

Hannie and Nancy clapped.

"That was great, Karen," Hannie said. "Very interesting. But maybe you should tell the folks at Stoneybrook Manor that you are friends with Bobby Martinez. That would be *really* interesting."

I could not tell whether Hannie knew I had lied. I had a feeling she suspected something.

I wondered if I should tell Hannie and Nancy about my lie. They would probably understand.

On the other hand, they might not think it was funny. I had lied to them along with everyone else. They might be mad at me.

I did not want my best friends to be mad at me.

Still, I did not want to tell any more lies than was necessary. (Especially since at least one person, Ricky, had already figured out that I was lying.) So there was no way I was going to repeat my Bobby Martinez Show and Share at Stoneybrook Manor.

"No," I said. "I think I will stick with 'My Two Families.' "

"But Karen — " Hannie started to say.

"Nope," I cut her off. " 'My Two Families' it is. I am not even going to discuss it."

Hannie shrugged. "Okay. Maybe you are right. Maybe it would be best if you did not talk about Bobby Martinez."

16

Stoneybrook Manor

On Wednesday, after lunch, Ms. Colman called together Omar Harris, Sara Ford, Jannie Gilbert, Ricky Torres, and me. Sara's mother, Mrs. Ford, was there to help too. (A substitute teacher stayed with the rest of the class while Ms. Colman came on the field trip with us.)

We gathered in front of the school. The photographs of my two families were safe in my book bag.

With us were our flowers in their deco- rated pots. Soon a school van pulled up, and we climbed in, being careful not to tip over our pots. We were on our way to Stoney-brook Manor.

I sat next to Sara Ford in the van. Sara is nice. (She had not once bugged me about knowing Bobby Martinez.) We chatted about this and that.

I was still not talking to Ricky, and he was still not talking to me. He had not told anybody that I had lied about knowing Bobby Martinez. But I could tell he was disappointed in me for lying to him. A couple of times I caught him looking at me. I could tell his feelings had been hurt. But I did not know what to say.

Finally the van pulled up to Stoneybrook Manor, and we all piled out. We carried our fancy potted flowers up the front steps and into the main hallway.

A great big banner said: WELCOME, MS. COLMAN'S CLASS!

A nice woman in a blue dress started talking to Ms. Colman and Mrs. Ford. In a room off the main hallway some people were watching television. A baseball game was on.

Omar, Ricky, and Jannie stood in the doorway to the room where the TV was on. Sara and I followed them. Ms. Colman and Mrs. Ford were still talking to the woman in the blue dress.

The announcer on TV was saying, "The Padres have the bases loaded, and Bobby Martinez is up at bat."

Just my luck! Of all the baseball players on all the teams in all the world, Bobby Martinez *would* have to be on TV when I walked into that room.

"Here is the pitch," said the TV announcer. "He swings!"

A loud *crack!* came from the TV, and then the roar of the crowd. The announcer sounded excited. "It is going, going, going . . . it is out of here! A grand slam home run for Bobby Martinez!"

Everyone who had been watching the game started whooping and shouting. A couple of men traded high fives.

Omar was jumping up and down and cheering too. As soon as the shouting stopped, Omar said loudly, "Bobby Martinez is so great! And you know what — Karen Brewer is practically best friends with him!"

Omar turned and pointed at me.

Sara, Ricky, and Jannie stepped back so the Stoneybrook Manor residents could get a better look at me.

A sickly smile spread across my face, and I gave a little wave. "Yup," I whispered. "That is me. Bobby Martinez's best friend."

17

Ricky to the Rescue?

Just then Ms. Colman said, "Okay, children, the residents are ready to receive our flowers and hear our presentations."

We followed Ms. Colman and Mrs. Ford down the hallway to another room. It was bigger than the TV room. In it were gathered about ten residents of Stoneybrook Manor. They were all smiling, and they waved hello to us when we entered. I waved and smiled back bravely. I was there to brighten their day.

First Ms. Colman asked us to present our

flowers to the residents. Since there were more residents than flowers, some of them did not get flowers. They did not seem to mind, though. The ones who got the flowers passed them around so that everyone could see. They were good sharers.

Next Ms. Colman asked us to give our Show and Share presentations.

Sara went first. She talked about her dog, Frederick. She explained that he is a dachshund. She showed a picture of him. He was pretty cute. Sara told a story about the time Frederick stole their Thanksgiving turkey off the dinner table. It was a funny story.

Then it was Omar's turn. He talked about his little sister. He brought in a painting they had made together. It was their handprints, side by side. Omar's little sister has a very small hand. The residents seemed to enjoy hearing about his sister.

Then Jannie showed some clip-on earrings that she had bought. "See?" she said. "They clip right on. I do not have to get my ears pierced. My mommy says I cannot have my ears pierced until I am in eighth grade anyway." She waggled her head back and forth to make her earrings sparkle.

It was hard for me to watch Ricky when it was his turn. I felt bad that I had lied to him. I wished I could apologize, but I did not think even an apology would help. It was too late to explain my lie.

Ricky talked about his Little League baseball team. He said he played right field, just like his hero, Bobby Martinez. (Ricky did not look at me when he mentioned Bobby's name.) He showed his Little League uniform shirt. It was green and said *Torres* across the back, above the number six. Ricky explained that Bobby Martinez's number was six too.

After the residents clapped for Bobby, it was my turn. I wished that Ricky had not gone on and on about Bobby Martinez.

I held up the photographs of my two families. "My name is Karen Brewer," I said. "Today I am going to talk about — "

"Bobby Martinez!" Omar interrupted me. "Talk about Bobby Martinez, Karen!"

"Um, no, I want to talk about — " I tried to say, but Jannie interrupted me this time.

"Karen knows Bobby Martinez," she said to one of the residents. "Her stepfather is Bobby's best friend."

"Really?" said the woman. "That is very interesting. Tell me, young lady," she said to me, "how did your stepfather come to know Bobby Martinez?"

"Yes, Karen," said Omar. "Tell us about Bobby — "

"Be quiet, Omar!" said Ricky. "Let Karen talk about what she wants to talk about. She does not have to talk about Bobby Martinez if she does not feel like it."

My mouth dropped open. I looked at Ricky. He was glaring at Omar. Then I looked at Ms. Colman. She was giving Ricky a Look of her own. She did not like it when one of her students told another kid to be quiet.

When I looked back at Ricky, he was look-

ing at the ground. I realized he was trying to help me. He did not want me to have to lie any more about knowing Bobby Martinez.

He was trying to come to my rescue.

Before I could say anything, another resident spoke up. He was an old man in a red-and-green-checked vest. He had a white beard.

"Why don't you tell us what you had planned to say," the old man said. "And when you are finished, you can tell us about Bobby Martinez too."

"Why don't you leave her alone?" Ricky said.

My mouth dropped open a second time. I could not believe what I had just heard.

"Ricky!" Ms. Colman said. "That is quite enough! I do not know what has gotten into you all of a sudden, but I will not stand for bad manners. Come with me."

Ricky and Ms. Colman started walking out of the room. This was terrible. Ricky was trying to save me from having to lie, and now Ms. Colman was angry at him.

94

"Wait!" I called. I could not let Ricky be punished instead of me. "Do not leave. I have something to say."

Tears welled up in my eyes. I was not sure whether they were there because of what I was about to say, or because of what Ricky had already done.

Either way, as soon as I said, "I do not know Bobby Martinez," I burst into tears.

A Bad Week

I never did get to talk about my two families. After I burst into tears, Ms. Colman brought me out of the room so we could talk in private.

I explained the truth to Ms. Colman. My first Show and Share, the one with Bobby Martinez's baseball card, had been a big lie.

Ms. Colman was disappointed in me for being dishonest, but she did not think I needed to be punished further. She said she felt my embarrassment at being caught in a lie was punishment enough.

I said okay, if she was sure.

Of course, after I explained the truth to Ms. Colman, I had to tell Omar, Sara, and Jannie too. I knew that by the end of the day, every kid in my class would know I had made up the Bobby Martinez story.

The next week was hard. Hannie and Nancy were not mad at me (well, not very, anyway). Hannie said she had suspected I was fibbing all along.

I tried to be especially nice to Ricky. I talked to him, smiled at him, paid extra attention to him. He seemed okay. He even smiled at me once. But I could tell things were not the same. He still did not trust me.

Omar and Jannie were madder at me than everyone else. Besides Ricky, they were the two biggest Bobby Martinez fans in the class. I tried to be extra nice to them too, though it was hard. I like Omar, but even when Jannie is not mad at me, she is a bit of a meanie-mo, not to mention being best friends with my best enemy, Pamela Harding.

All week Pamela went out of her way to make fun of me.

"Ooh, Karen," she said. "I heard your uncle, Pete Sampras, just won another tennis tournament."

Ha-ha.

"Karen," Pamela said. "Shaquille O'Neal is making a new movie. Maybe you can get a part in it. He is your godfather, isn't he?"

Ha-ha-ha.

"Karen," said Pamela, "the U.S. women's gymnastics team is giving an exhibition in New York this weekend. Maybe you can get our class free tickets, since they are seven of your very closest friends."

Ha-ha-ha-ha. I was not laughing.

At least Mommy was nice about what had happened. Ms. Colman had told me that I should tell my parents about what I had done. So I did. Mommy and I had a long talk about honesty. (I am ashamed to admit it, but we have had this talk before.) Then she hugged me and told me she loved me. I said I loved her too. (I was being very honest.)

Mommy did say, though, that I should tell Charlie that I had tricked him. I had to apologize to Charlie.

I called him on the phone.

"Hello, Charlie?" I said. "This is Karen."

"Hi, Karen," said Charlie. "What can I do for you?"

"Charlie, I need to say I am sorry," I said. "Remember on the day of the cookout, when I asked you to sign Bobby Martinez's name on that baseball?"

"Sure," Charlie said.

I told Charlie the whole story, about wanting to get a signed ball for Ricky and pretending the one Charlie had signed was real.

"So that is what I did," I said. "I am very sorry I tricked you, Charlie."

Charlie was laughing. (He had started laughing about halfway through my story.)

"Karen, you are too much," he said. "There is no trouble you will not get yourself into, is there?"

"I am not sure," I said. "It is definitely possible that there is trouble that I would not get myself into. But I have not found it yet."

Charlie laughed. "Well, I forgive you. Just do not trick me that way again, okay?"

"Okay," I said happily.

"Next time," said Charlie, "trick Sam instead."

"Oh, um, right. Okay. 'Bye."

"Good-bye," said Charlie.

Well, that had not been too bad. Charlie had been much nicer about it than I had expected.

19

Karen's Letter

It was Saturday afternoon. I was in the living room, trying to read a book. I was trying, but not succeeding.

I was not succeeding because Andrew was upstairs in his room playing the kazoo. As usual. I had made up new words to the tune he was playing. They went like this:

This old Andrew
He plays kazoo.

He plays kazoo and I say boo
And bullfrogs, pollywogs, give a girl a break.
This little brother will not do.

I sang the words to myself over and over. I could not concentrate on what I was trying to read.

"Karen," Mommy called. "There is a letter in the mail for you."

"For me?" I leaped off the couch and ran to the front hall. I love getting mail. Maybe it was from my pen pal, Maxie, in New York.

Mommy handed me the envelope. I looked at the return address. It said *San Diego Padres.*

Oh my gosh! Suddenly I remembered the letter I had written Bobby Martinez. He had written back!

Carefully I opened the envelope (I did not want to ruin it by ripping it) and took out the letter.

It said:

Dear Fan,

Thank you very much for your kind words. It is fans like you who make the game worth playing. Every time my teammates and I step on the field, we give one hundred percent. With the enthusiastic support of the best fans in baseball, I am sure we will have another great season.

Sincerely,

Bobby Martinez

Wow! Bobby Martinez said I made the game worth playing.

"Look at this, Mommy!" I said. I handed her the letter. "Bobby took the time to sit down and write me himself."

Mommy read the letter. Then she said, "This is a very nice letter, Karen. But I do not think Bobby typed it up just for you. It is a form letter. I think he sends these out to everyone who writes to him."

"Oh," I said. I was crushed. Just a form letter.

Then Mommy held the letter close to her face. "But you know, the signature looks real. I do not think it was printed on a machine. I think you may have a real autograph here."

"Really?" I said. Suddenly I knew what I had to do with the letter. "Mommy, I need to go to the baseball card shop at the mall right away. I have to find out for sure if the signature is really Bobby's."

"Ricky, I would like to apologize one last time," I said on Monday morning.

"You have already said you are sorry," Ricky replied.

"I know. But I want you to know I really, really am sorry I lied to you. And — " I smiled. "I have something to show you."

"Show me?" Ricky asked. "What is it?"

I took the envelope from behind my back and gave it to him.

"Ta-daaa!" I said.

Ricky took the letter out, unfolded it, and read it.

"Where did you get this?" he asked. "Is it real? Did Bobby really write this?"

"I got it in the mail," I said. "Yes, it is real. And Bobby sort of wrote it. I had written him a fan letter. Mommy says this is the form letter he sends everyone who writes to him. But," I said importantly, "the signature is real. I had it checked at the card shop. It is a genuine Bobby Martinez autograph."

Ricky stared at the letter he was holding. I wondered if he thought I was lying again.

"I am telling the truth this time," I said. "It really is a Bobby Martinez autograph."

"I know," said Ricky. "I believe you. I was just looking at it. It is awesome."

"Yes, it is awesome," I said. "And it is yours."

"Mine? You are giving it to me?"

I nodded. "Yup. I promised to get you a Bobby Martinez autograph. So here it is."

"Gee, thanks, Karen!" said Ricky.

"You are welcome. And I want to thank you too for trying to help me at Stoneybrook Manor. It was very nice of you."

"Aw, it was nothing," said Ricky. He looked down and kicked at a pebble near his toe. He was blushing. He looked up at me and smiled.

I could feel myself blushing a little too as I smiled back.

20

Little-House Kazoo Band

I was still in a good mood when I got home that afternoon. I thought that nothing could bring me down. Except —

This old Andrew
He plays kazoo.
He plays kazoo and I say boo
And bullfrogs, pollywogs . . .

The sound of the kazoo was louder than ever. And it was not coming from Andrew's room upstairs. It was coming from the kitchen.

"What is going on here?" I shouted, charging into the kitchen.

To my horror, I saw Andrew humming into his kazoo — and with him were Mommy, Seth, and Merry. And Mommy and Seth were humming into kazoos too!

"What — what — what?" I sputtered. "What are you doing home?" I asked Mommy and Seth. "Why is Andrew playing his kazoo in the kitchen? And why are you two playing with him?" I stared at them in disbelief.

Andrew, Mommy, and Seth stopped kazooing. (Thank goodness!)

"I will be right back," Merry said. She went into the living room.

"We were both having slow days at work today," Mommy said to me. "So we decided to come home early. And Seth picked up these kazoos for us."

108

"But . . . why?" I asked. "One kazoo in the house is more than enough."

"Oh, come on, Karen," said Seth. "Do not be a fuddy-duddy. I bought one for you too." He took yet another kazoo out of his pocket and held it up for me.

Well! No one calls *me* a fuddy-duddy! I took the kazoo and hummed into it experimentally: *Hrrrmmmm!*

Kind of neat, I had to admit. It tickled my lips.

"If you cannot beat them, join them," said Seth. "Right, Karen?"

Before I had a chance to reply, Merry came back into the kitchen. She was carrying a little electronic keyboard.

"I brought this to accompany your kazoo concert," Merry explained. She flipped a switch and pressed some keys. It sounded just like a piano!

"So what shall we play?" asked Mommy.

"How about 'This Old Man'?" Andrew suggested.

"No!" I cried. "Anything but that!"

Seth laughed. "Okay. How about 'She'll Be Comin' Round the Mountain'? I think we all know that tune."

Merry waved her hands like a conductor, and we started playing "She'll Be Comin' Round the Mountain."

It sounded great! Pretty soon Merry stopped conducting and joined in with her keyboard. The Little-House Kazoo Band was in full swing:

She'll be comin' round the mountain
She'll be comin' round the mountain
She'll be comin' round the mountain when
she comes!

L. GODWIN

About the Author

ANN M. MARTIN lives in New York City and loves animals, especially cats. She has two cats of her own, Gussie and Woody.

Other books by Ann M. Martin that you might enjoy are *Stage Fright; Me and Katie (the Pest);* and the books in *The Baby-sitters Club* series.

Ann likes ice cream and *I Love Lucy*. And she has her own little sister, whose name is Jane.

Little Sister

Don't miss #110

KAREN'S SWIM MEET

"Okay, kids! Get ready for the freestyle," called Coach Carson.

I took off my shorts and T-shirt. Then I stuffed my hair in my cap and put on my goggles. I already knew that freestyle and crawl are two names for the same stroke. I am good at it.

"Swim next to me," whispered Terri.

I stood in the lane next to Terri's and waited for the starting whistle.

"Fifteen seconds to go," called our coach.

The whistle blew. I swam up the lane, then back. Up the lane, then back. I listened for the whistle again. But I did not hear it. I kept going. Up the lane, then back. I was swimming a long time and did not hear the whistle. I thought maybe I had water in my ears and could not hear it. But everyone else was still swimming too. Up the lane, then back. I swam back and forth so many times I lost count. Finally the whistle blew.

Terri was the last one to reach the wall again. She was huffing and puffing.

"We will rest for thirty seconds, then do the backstroke," said Coach Carson.

Terri looked at me and made a face. I did not have a chance to say anything before the whistle blew again.

I am not very good at the backstroke. But I could keep up. We swam for a long time again. Then we did the breaststroke. Then we used kickboards. Finally practice was over.

"See you tomorrow. Nine o'clock sharp. Go, team, go!" said Coach Carson.

I was tired but excited about swimming.

"This was fun!" I said to Terri.

She did not think so. She looked at me and rolled her eyes.

BABY-SITTERS™

Little Sister

by Ann M. Martin
author of The Baby-sitters Club®

❏ MQ44300-3 #1	Karen's Witch	$2.95
❏ MQ44258-9 #5	Karen's School Picture	$2.95
❏ MQ43651-1 #10	Karen's Grandmothers	$2.95
❏ MQ43645-7 #15	Karen's in Love	$2.95
❏ MQ44823-4 #20	Karen's Carnival	$2.95
❏ MQ44831-5 #25	Karen's Pen Pal	$2.95
❏ MQ44830-7 #26	Karen's Ducklings	$2.95
❏ MQ44829-3 #27	Karen's Big Joke	$2.95
❏ MQ44828-5 #28	Karen's Tea Party	$2.95
❏ MQ44825-0 #29	Karen's Cartwheel	$2.75
❏ MQ45645-8 #30	Karen's Kittens	$2.95
❏ MQ45646-6 #31	Karen's Bully	$2.95
❏ MQ45647-4 #32	Karen's Pumpkin Patch	$2.95
❏ MQ45648-2 #33	Karen's Secret	$2.95
❏ MQ45650-4 #34	Karen's Snow Day	$2.95
❏ MQ45652-0 #35	Karen's Doll Hospital	$2.95
❏ MQ45651-2 #36	Karen's New Friend	$2.95
❏ MQ45653-9 #37	Karen's Tuba	$2.95
❏ MQ45655-5 #38	Karen's Big Lie	$2.95
❏ MQ45654-7 #39	Karen's Wedding	$2.95
❏ MQ47040-X #40	Karen's Newspaper	$2.95
❏ MQ47041-8 #41	Karen's School	$2.95
❏ MQ47042-6 #42	Karen's Pizza Party	$2.95
❏ MQ46912-6 #43	Karen's Toothache	$2.95
❏ MQ47043-4 #44	Karen's Big Weekend	$2.95
❏ MQ47044-2 #45	Karen's Twin	$2.95
❏ MQ47045-0 #46	Karen's Baby-sitter	$2.95
❏ MQ46913-4 #47	Karen's Kite	$2.95
❏ MQ47046-9 #48	Karen's Two Families	$2.95
❏ MQ47047-7 #49	Karen's Stepmother	$2.95
❏ MQ47048-5 #50	Karen's Lucky Penny	$2.95
❏ MQ48230-0 #55	Karen's Magician	$2.95
❏ MQ48305-6 #60	Karen's Pony	$2.95
❏ MQ25998-9 #65	Karen's Toys	$2.95
❏ MQ26279-3 #66	Karen's Monsters	$2.95
❏ MQ26024-3 #67	Karen's Turkey Day	$2.95
❏ MQ26025-1 #68	Karen's Angel	$2.95
❏ MQ26193-2 #69	Karen's Big Sister	$2.95
❏ MQ26280-7 #70	Karen's Grandad	$2.95
❏ MQ26194-0 #71	Karen's Island Adventure	$2.95
❏ MQ26195-9 #72	Karen's New Puppy	$2.95
❏ MQ26301-3 #73	Karen's Dinosaur	$2.95
❏ MQ26214-9 #74	Karen's Softball Mystery	$2.95
❏ MQ69183-X #75	Karen's County Fair	$2.95
❏ MQ69184-8 #76	Karen's Magic Garden	$2.95
❏ MQ69185-6 #77	Karen's School Surprise	$2.99
❏ MQ69186-4 #78	Karen's Half Birthday	$2.99
❏ MQ69187-2 #79	Karen's Big Fight	$2.99

More Titles... ➡